The Grumpy Guidebook

The Grumpy Guidebook

A Step-By-Step Guide Through the Transition from Middle-Aged and Successful to Old and Grumpy

Old & Grumpy, LLC
Vincent Fratto and Michael Fayol

Contents

Prologue

Welcome you, my fellow curmudgeon, to the start of your transition, your journey from middle-aged and successful to old and grumpy, and you, sir, deserve a hearty congratulations! You have spent a lifetime in traffic, in a cubical or retail store, a restaurant or service garage, and have piled up professional success after success and failure after failure (for what is success with no failure to compare it to?). Whatever your path, you have done it, all your years of dealing with other people's b.s. has led to this inevitable statement—you're old now and let's face it, kind of grumpy.

Don't recoil from that statement, be proud, you should be! Here you find yourself on the precipice of grumpy greatness, like the elders that have come before you. But you are new here and unsure of yourself, anxious about how to proceed with this natural next step in your age evolution. Here lies before you the eternal question; How do I hone my grumpy skills for the next chapter of my life to make my grumpy years as successful as my professional years?

Have no fear, my grumpy grasshopper, I will lead you through the illuminating journey of becoming a grumpy old man! I will walk you through in great specificity and detail how to master all aspects of grumpy greatness so that when your time on this crazy blue marble is done, others will think of you, saying, "Boy, he sure was grumpy," and what more can a man ask for in a legacy?!

In our first chapter, we shall embark on an enlightening adventure, exploring the subtle art of grumpy facial expressions. So, gather your furrowed brows and prepare to perfect that world-class scowl!

VOLUME 1
GRUMPY EXPRESSIONS

CHAPTER 1:
The Art of Grumpy Facial Expressions

Mastering the Eyebrow Raise

Ah, the eyebrow raise. An indispensable tool in the arsenal of any self-respecting grump. With just a subtle lift of the brow, we can convey a multitude of emotions without uttering a single word. It is the silent language of disapproval, the universal signal of disdain, and our secret weapon in the battle against cheerful exuberance.

Now, you might wonder, why should we bother perfecting this particular maneuver? Well, my friend, the answer lies in the sheer satisfaction of watching others squirm under the weight of our withering gaze. It's the unspoken power that accompanies a perfectly executed eyebrow raise, leaving unsuspecting souls questioning their life choices, their fashion sense, and, if done correctly, their very existence.

But fear not, for I shall guide you through the intricacies of this grumpy art form. First, find yourself a mirror, for self-reflection is the cornerstone of our journey. Stand before it, brow furrowed, face set in a determined scowl, and let us begin.

The Foundation

To commence our training, let's start with the basics. Relax your facial muscles and take a deep breath, take a second, and think back to your last trip to the supermarket and a random fool you had to suffer through. Any commonplace idiot will do, like that Grade A moron in the produce section weighing one organic avocado vs the other in exaggerated up and down arm motions like it actually makes a difference. He's perfect, keep him in mind. Now, with that food for thought, raise one eyebrow slowly, as if effortlessly challenging the world to meet your unimpressed gaze. Hold it there for a moment, keep it steady, good, allow the dissatisfaction to seep into your very being. Excellent, well done! Repeat this exercise with the other brow, ensuring both eyebrows receive equal attention. It's important not to form a dominant brow (be it left or right), that will throw off the formation of your forehead wrinkles, and no one wants that.

Mastering the Subtleties

Remember, my grumpy apprentice, subtlety is key, for in the realm of grumpy expressions, less is often more. The true master of subtleties understands the power of restraint and the art of the slight raise, that fractional lift that conveys volumes without overt effort. It is in the delicate balance between minimal movement and profound impact that the essence of grumpy expressions lie. Practice in front of your mirror with diligence, honing your ability to execute these subtle gestures with precision. Keep your movements measured and controlled, like a salty maestro conducting an orchestra of grumpy emotions. Just as a skilled conductor guides each section of the orchestra to create a harmonious symphony, so too must you orchestrate a captivating performance of agitation and discontent.

Well done, always remember; through the gentle elevation of an eyebrow, you can communicate skepticism, silently questioning the absurdity that surrounds you. With a barely perceptible narrowing of your eyes, you cast a shadow of suspicion upon those fools who dare to cross your grumpy path. These nuanced movements, when executed with the right amount of finesse, serve as the brushstrokes that paint a vivid portrait of your inner turmoil and discontentment.

Don't go overboard here, it is not the grand theatrics that define a true grumpy master but the subtle and controlled expressions that leave others unsettled with the folly of their ways. It is the unspoken language of your beautifully grumpy soul, capable of conveying more than a thousand words ever could. That is the true essence of the subtle brow raise.

Advanced Variations

Now that you have grasped the fundamentals, let us embark on a journey through the advanced spectrum of emotions your eyebrow raise can masterfully convey. Prepare yourself for an exploration of grumpy expressions that will elevate your eyebrow game to new heights. Let's take a moment here to stretch your face—we aren't spring chickens anymore, and the last thing we want is a trip to the ER with a world-class face cramp. While that might help your overall grump level, it's not worth it.

Okay, all stretched and loose, now we are ready for some advanced level brow movements.

Exploring beyond the realm of the ordinary, brace yourself for the epic unveiling of "The Browlift Cataclysm." This look is honed through countless hours of eye-rolling at the follies of humanity. This look requires raising both brows in perfect unison with a stone-cold stern expression glued to your face, your mouth perfectly parallel to your raising brows. As your brows ascend as one, the world around you becomes the recipient of your delicate yet demonstrative admonishment, for its

PRO TIP:

add a slight smirk at the same time to really drive it home. Angle your smirk to the same side as the raised brow

lack of sophistication is unworthy of your admiration. This expression exudes an aura of refined indifference, silently proclaiming your disapproval and disdain with resounding clarity.

*NOTE THE KNOWING SMIRK

Next, take a moment to look around you to ensure your surroundings are safe and secure before we move on to "The Sarcastic Arch of Condemnation," a grandiose spectacle that transcends mere eyebrow raises. For this execution, focus only on a single brow and rapidly ascend it, not in a mere display of disdain but in a sardonic dance of mockery. This audacious maneuver showcases your unparalleled wit and keen awareness of the absurdities that engulf us all. As your brow ascends, add a dash subtle smirk, strictly on the same side as the raised brow, which will incite a ripple of disbelief reverberating through onlookers like a shockwave, casting doubt upon their own rationality and questioning the very essence of their taste. "The Sarcastic Arch of Condemnation" is a tour de force, a theatrical masterpiece that intertwines grumpy prowess with the art of subtle mockery. It is an expression that demands attention, a gesture that serves as a wake-up call to the delusions of society. With this singular movement, you become the curator of wit, the maestro of irony, and the herald of truth. Embrace the power it bestows upon you and revel in the bewilderment of those who are privileged enough to witness this remarkable feat of your artisanal mastery of grump.

Finally, behold as we unveil the captivating marvel known as "The Summit of Elevated Scorn," a technique that demands unwavering precision, finesse, and undivided attention. This extraordinary expression is reserved for the elite grumpy connoisseurs and requires precise control over each muscle fiber involved in the elevation of a single brow. Pay attention to the angle now, ensure it is sharp yet refined, project a profound sense of confident authority. Allow the situation to dictate the speed of said raise. Practice maintaining a relaxed facial expression throughout while focusing solely on the movement of your eyebrow. As your brow powerfully ascends, it serves as a lofty proclamation, an insignia of your elevated status above the mundane and extraordinarily ridiculous alike. In that fleeting moment, you become the epitome of discerning judgment, casting your critical gaze upon the world with a regal air.

When done right, "The Summit of Elevated Scorn" transcends the realm of man, exuding an air of Mount Olympus-level of superiority that leaves no room for doubt. With impeccable control, a dash of panache, and the might of Zeus himself, you declare your intellectual prowess, positioning yourself as a distinguished Lord of Refined Grumpiness who is second to none.

You are now at the pinnacle of grumpy expressions, an artform mastered by us chosen few who possess the audacity to stand above the fray. With this singular gesture, you navigate the heights of refined grumpiness, surveying the lesser beings from your lofty perch as your face screams out 'begone, vile mortals!'

That was tough, but we made it through to the other side! Pat yourself on the back, this is really advanced-level stuff we are dealing with here. Take a breath and get a drink if you need before we move on.

Fine-Tuning and Personalization

Well done, my grumpy brother, we have arrived at a pivotal moment in your journey toward grumpy enlightenment. This is where the true artistry of the grumpy expression unfolds—the realm of fine-tuning and personalization. As with any art form, the eyebrow raise is an expression of your individuality, a canvas upon which you leave your distinct grumpy fingerprint. Now is the time to embrace your unique style, to experiment with your own variations, and to refine your grumpy persona.

No two grumpy individuals are alike, and each of you possesses a singular essence that sets you apart from the rest. As you embark on the exploration of eyebrow raises, let your creativity flourish—just have fun with it! Experiment with angles, intensities, and speeds, and observe how each subtle adjustment transforms the message conveyed by your lifted brow. Beware though, a little goes a long way here. Add a little too much flair to "The Browlift Cataclysm," for example, and empires fall. This look was the true reason Rome fell, so use it well but beware of its power.

Take inspiration from the grumpy greats who have come before you, but do not be confined by their styles. Instead, infuse their wisdom with your personal touch, combining their techniques with your own idiosyncrasies. In doing so, you will cultivate a style that is entirely yours—one that carries the weight of your grumpy experiences and the depths of your discernment. As you embark on your journey of fine-tuning and personalization, remember that grumpiness is an ever-evolving art. Embrace the joy of exploration, the delight in discovering new expressions that perfectly encapsulate your exasperation. Allow your grumpy persona to grow, to adapt, and to surprise even yourself.

And so, gentlemen, let us forge ahead with unwavering determination. Hone your eyebrow raises, seek out the subtleties that resonate with your soul, and sculpt your grumpy identity with purpose and conviction. In this realm of personalization, you have the power to create a legacy—a legacy of grumpiness that reflects the true essence of who you are.

In Conclusion

Congratulations, my fellow grump-in-the-making! You have taken your first steps toward becoming a master of grumpy facial expressions. Through dedicated practice and a commitment to embracing your inner curmudgeon, you will forge a path to grumpy enlightenment, a course paved with scowls and raised eyebrows. As you continue your journey, remember that grumpiness is a talent that evolves with age. With each passing day, you will discover new depths of grumpiness within you, polishing your skills and perfecting your expressions is a key part of the transition from middle aged and successful to old and grumpy.

Let us not forget that grumpiness is not an end in itself. It is a means to an end, a tool to navigate the trials and tribulations of life with a touch of humor and a dash of irreverence. It is a reminder to never take ourselves too seriously, to find joy in the absurdity of the world around us.

So, my grumpy comrade, as we conclude this introductory chapter, let us raise our eyebrows in unison, basking in the collective grumpiness that binds us together. May your scowls grow deeper, your eye-rolls sharper, and your wit be honed to a sharp edge. And always remember, a well-executed grumpy expression is worth a thousand words.

In the next chapter, we shall delve into the art of perfecting the grumpy sigh, a cornerstone of our repertoire. Prepare yourselves, for a world of exasperation awaits. Until then, my fellow grump, embrace your crotchetiness and wear it proudly. Onward we march, toward a future filled with wrinkled brows and witty retorts!

CHAPTER 2:
The Grumpy Sigh – Exhaling Dissatisfaction

With the mastery of the Grumpy Facial Expressions in our back pocket, let us now gather around and immerse ourselves in the captivating realm of the grumpy sigh. In the following pages, you discover how to employ a symphony of frustration, a sonata of annoyance, giving testament to the weariness that resides deep within our grumpy souls. In this chapter, we shall embark on a profound journey, unravelling the intricate components that give birth to the grumpy sigh and exploring the vast emotions it embodies. Brace yourself, my comrade, for we are about to embark on a harmonic expedition that will resonate with the very essence of our grumpiness.

The grumpy sigh is not a mere exhale of air but a profound expression of our exasperation, a release of pent-up frustration that resonates through our being. It carries the weight of countless annoyances and grievances, drawing upon a lifetime of encounters with the irritating aspects of the world.

To truly master the art of the grumpy sigh, we must first understand its intricate components. The grumpy sigh is a language of its own, spoken by countless grumpy souls throughout the ages. It is a language that transcends words, an ancient dialect understood by our fellow grumps. With each sigh, we communicate our shared frustration, our weariness with the world's absurdities, and our longing for a simpler, more sensible existence. It is a sigh that echoes the sentiments of grumpy minds across generations, binding us together in a harmonious chorus of discontent.

So, my grumpy brother, let us embrace the grumpy sigh in all its glory as we explore its nuances, practice its cadence, and unleash its power upon the world.

Step 1: The Breath of Exasperation

A grumpy sigh is not merely a casual exhalation; it is a deliberate and purposeful act of releasing pent-up frustration upon a simpleton in your presence. To truly master the art of the grumpy sigh, we must begin with the breath—the foundation upon which our discontentment rests.

Close your eyes and take a deep breath, pull again from a random fool as food for your grumpiness. Now, inhale slowly, allowing the air to fill your lungs with the weight of the world's follies. Feel the heaviness settle upon your shoulders, an invisible burden that only we, the grumpy few, carry. As you breathe in, let the essence of your grumpiness permeate every fiber of your being. Absorb the countless irritations, the nonsensical behaviors, and the ludicrous inconveniences that surround us. Allow them to merge and mingle with your inner grump, creating a concentrated swirling vortex of exasperation within you (pro tip: This is not a passive inhalation but an active absorption of all that fuels your grumpy soul).

Good, very good. Now, as you reach the peak of inhalation, hold that breath for a brief moment, savoring the anticipation of what is to come. The air within you is now charged with the energy of grumpiness, ready to be unleashed. The breath of exasperation sets the stage for the grand performance of your grumpy sigh, the masterful release of discontent.

Step 2: The Release of Discontent

Now comes the climactic moment of truth—the release of our discontent. With a deliberate exhalation (and let's be honest; a bit of a flair for the dramatic) that seems to stretch on for an eternity, let out a sigh that speaks volumes of your discontent. It should be a sigh so profound, so magnificently elongated, that it transcends the boundaries of trivial matters such as 'time and space' and becomes the embodiment of your weariness, irritation, and resignation upon the sigh's recipient.

The sound should resonate through the air, as if the universe itself pauses to listen to your grumpy proclamation. Let it be a sigh that encapsulates the collective frustration of grumpy souls across eons. A sigh so deep and lengthy that it surpasses the mere limitations of human understanding. Allow it to stretch out, like a lazy cat luxuriating in the warmth of a sunbeam. You know you are doing it right when the sigh meanders through the air, weaving its way into the consciousness of all who have the privilege of hearing it!

Expressive Variations

Like a grumpy maestro, you have the power to imbue your sigh with different emotions and meanings. Let us explore some expressive variations to elevate your grumpy sigh's game.

The "Heavyweight Sigh"

HEAVYWEIGHT SIGH

Picture yourself carrying the weight of the world on your shoulders, because, in all honesty, this is our duty as a grump. Once you have the entire earth fixed upon your back, let out a sigh that conveys the burden of your existence, making others acutely aware of the struggles that accompany your grumpy wisdom—whether they asked for it or not. As the Heavyweight Sigh escapes your lips, it fills the space around you with a thick, tangible presence. It hangs in the air, enveloping those nearby in its aura of grumpy authenticity. The sound should be deep and resonant, conveying the weight of your existence with each passing second. It should echo through the room, a solemn reminder of the battles fought and the scars earned. The Heavyweight Sigh can be enjoyed in a group of others, say at a family gathering or a movie theater, or by yourself in a street café or walking around in your town's square. Sometimes it's nice simply to let out a Heavyweight sigh even when alone, unprovoked. It has a satisfying melody that sooths the soul upon release.

The "Utter Disbelief Sigh"

DISBELIEF SIGH

Encounter an act of sheer stupidity? Exhale a sigh that communicates your utter disbelief at the lack of common sense and elegance in the world. Through this combined gesture, you assert your place as a grumpy sage, witnessing the absurdities of the world with a critical eye and unapologetic candor. It is a reminder that you are old, dammit, and expressing your disdain for the lack of class you see before you is your privileged duty.

PRO TIP:

combine this with an eyeroll for maximum effect and efficiency.

The "Pitying Sigh"

PITYING SIGH

Witness someone making foolish choices? Let out a sigh that carries an undertone of pity, as if silently acknowledging their impending regret. This sigh speaks volumes without uttering a single word. Imagine the scene unfolding before your eyes—a person confidently embarking on a path of folly, oblivious to the consequences that lie ahead. It could be a friend making ill-advised financial decisions or a colleague pursuing a doomed romantic entanglement. Regardless of the specific ridiculous circumstance, your grumpy wisdom allows you to see the inevitable outcome with utmost clarity, and it is your duty as resident grumpy old man to express it with a Pitying Sigh. This sigh serves as a non-verbal cue, inviting the person to reconsider their choices and potentially course-correct before it's too late. It acts as a silent guardian, offering a gentle nudge toward the path of wisdom that you can clearly see before them.

Timing and Delivery

Timing is everything when it comes to the grumpy sigh. It must be executed with impeccable precision to maximize its impact. Choose your moments wisely, my grumpy disciple. Let the sigh escape just as someone utters a particularly ridiculous statement or when faced with yet another mind-numbing inconvenience from yet another fool. Now is your time to strike!

Remember, the grumpy sigh is not a one-size-fits-all solution. It should be meticulously crafted and tailored to fit each unique situation, each exasperating annoyance, and each unfortunate person who has the misfortune of crossing your grumpy path. In the grand tapestry of grumpiness, your sigh becomes a personalized brushstroke, painting a vivid picture of your discontent and dissatisfaction with others. Always consider the individuals on the receiving end of the sigh as well. Are they oblivious souls who require a sigh dripping with sarcasm and biting irony? Or are they more receptive to a sigh tinged with a touch of empathy and understanding? Tailor your grumpy sigh to elicit the desired response—a momentary pause, a pang of guilt, or a glimmer of self-awareness. Remember, you are the grumpy elder statesman, the sigh recipient will look to you for your grumpy guidance and direction, so don't be shy to give it to them in spades.

Advancing your Grumpy sigh

The grumpy sigh might be a simple two-step process, but as any discerning grumpster knows, the journey to perfection is an un-yielding one. There are still greater heights to be attained, and the grumpy sigh is all about a strong finish so you can bask in your sigh's glory. This is where you infuse your sigh with an aura of pure grumpy brilliance to take it to a whole new level. In this advanced stage, your sighs become more than just exhalations of discontent; they become masterpieces of grumpiness that leave an indelible mark on all who encounter them.

Let's explore a few tried and true finishing moves. This is by no means a complete list but rather a few highlights for you to get your grumpy juices flowing.

The Echoing Resonance

Unleash the power of your grumpy sighs by creating an echoing resonance that reverberates through the corridors of frustration. As you release your sigh, allow it to bounce off the walls of indifference, amplifying its impact and making your discontent heard far and wide. Let the echoes of your sigh linger in the air, serving as a haunting reminder of your grumpy presence and leaving a lasting impression on those within earshot.

The Sigh-Fueled Rant

Elevate your grumpy sighs to new heights by transforming them into powerful fuel for a grumpy rant. After exhaling your sigh of discontent, let the words flow with precision and eloquence, de-livering a scathing commentary on the absurdities of life. This well-orchestrated blend of sighs and speech will leave your audience astounded by your grumpy eloquence.

The Sigh Signature

Just as a painter signs their masterpiece, so too must you leave your mark on the world with your signature grumpy sigh. Develop a unique sigh that becomes your calling card, a sigh so distinctive that it is recognized as yours alone. Let your sigh serve as a badge of honor, declaring your status as a true artisan of grumpiness.

CHAPTER 3:
The Art of Grumpy Commentary – Verbal Volleys of Wit

B efore we embark on this journey, it is my responsibility to give a word of caution: the realm of grumpy commentary holds an intoxicating power that few can resist. We must proceed carefully into this domain, where a captivating warning prevails. Brace yourself, for within this chapter lies the instructions for you to become a true artisan of grumpy commentary and witty banter.

Let us venture together now, you and I, into this enchanting world where the art of crafting witty verbal volleys takes center stage. Here, your words will become the tool of your grumpy expression, allowing you to convey your dissatisfaction with unrivaled precision. Prepare to unleash your linguistic prowess and engage in the delightful dance of grumpy banter so your growing grumpiness is not only felt and seen but heard.

You must understand that the true power of grumpy commentary lies not only in the words we choose but also in the way we deliver them. As with Grumpy Facial Expressions and Grumpy Sighs, timing is crucial, for a well-timed quip can land with devastating effect, leaving our targets speechless and our fellow grumps in awe of our command of grumpy wit.

Follow my lead, and I will help you to refine your linguistic skills, sharpening your tongue and linguistic dexterity to become a true master of grumpy wit. Now we take our first steps into the realm of subtle wordplay, embracing puns, double entendres, and clever phrasing to inject a touch of grumpy whimsy into our everyday conversation.

Grumpy Commentary in Everyday Life

Incorporate grumpy commentary into your everyday exchanges, transforming mundane conversations into moments of grumpy delight. Inject yourself, forcefully if you must, into foolish and questionable opinions with carefully crafted remarks that leave no doubt about your grumpy stance. Wasn't there at the start of the conversation? Not sure exactly what the conversation is about? Who cares? Inject anyway, it's your grumpy right!

Remember, the goal is not to foster positive change or win people over, that time has passed. Your aim is to assert your grumpy presence and make yourself heard in every conversation. Let your words carry the weight of your grumpy disposition. They have the power to shape the narrative and leave a lasting impression that will reverberate long after the conversation is over.

Grumpy commentary is not confined to formal settings or structured conversations; it has the power to permeate the very fabric of your everyday life, becoming an integral part of your grumpy persona. Take the opportunity in every interaction to unleash your grumpy wit and make your voice heard. Practice at home as often as possible—just don't ruffle your significant other, you'd be on your own, I can't help you there. This book is about successfully navigating the transition to becoming grumpy, not navigating the impossible. Hey... actually, if you're writing a book on that subject, or know of one, send it my way. I can certainly use the help in that regard!

The Elements of Grumpy Commentary

Grumpy commentary is more than a mere exchange of words. It is an intricate dance, a ballet of sharp wit and acerbic humor. To master this art, we must first understand its fundamental elements.

The 1st Element: Timing and Delivery

Ah, timing and delivery—the twin pillars upon which grumpy conversations are built. Let's practice now; imagine yourself in a conversation, your grumpy senses tingling with anticipation—now is the time to strike. Let the words linger in the air to build suspense like a magician holding the final card. Then, with the precision of a skilled surgeon, unleash your grumpy remark. It should hit its target with the force of a grumpy thunderbolt, leaving your audience hanging on the edge of their seats, yearning for more grumpy brilliance.

Timing is the secret ingredient that separates the amateurs from the true grumpy masters. It's like delivering the perfect punchline, but instead of laughter, you aim for a chorus of grumpy acknowledgment. So, be patient, savor the moment, it's important not to rush it. When you unleash your grumpy charm at just the right instant and strike with impeccable timing, the impact will be nothing short of grumpy magic.

Don't forget to stick your delivery as well; it's equally important. Your tone of voice should reflect the very essence of your grumpiness. Picture it as a blend of weary resignation, subtle irritation, and a pinch of dry sarcasm. Let your words drip with the weight of your discontentment, delivered with a deadpan expression that adds an extra layer of grumpy charm. Remember, it's not just what you say but how you say it that amplifies the impact of your grumpy commentary. Pro tip: Mix in advanced facial expressions or start with a grumpy sigh to really separate yourself.

The 2nd Element: Satire and Irony

Now we get to the real meat and potatoes of Grumpy Conversation, where satire and irony reign supreme. Stand before your trusty mirror again... what do you mean you're not at your mirror. Okay, I'll give you a minute to walk there. Geez, don't let me keep you... okay, good (wow, you walk slowly). Right, let's jump back into this. You took too long, and I lost my place. Where were we? Ah, right! Timing and Delivery! Wait, hold on, I think we already did that. Satire and irony, that's it! Next time try to be prepared. Okay. Satire and Irony. Prepare to unlock the full potential of your grumpy wit.

Mastering the art of delivering biting remarks that will leave others both belittled and enlightened. This is not a casual endeavor, mind you—it requires dedication and finesse. You've gotten this far into this book, so you're certainly dedicated, I'll give you that; finesse, though, well, that still remains to be seen, but I believe in you.

PRO TIP:

A simple "yeah" or "Yup" delivered just right is worth more than any sentence.

So, gaze at your reflection, summoning the spirit of sarcasm that lies within. Craft your words with precision, stripping away the mask of societal absurdities to expose the contradictions and follies that surround us. Now, with a mischievous glint in your eye, let your words dance with playful venom. Deliver your remarks with impeccable timing and a tone that brims with ironic amusement. Observe how your reflection reacts, and let it be your guide. As you stand there, in front of your mirror, explore the delightful tension between what is said and what is meant; how the subtle nuances of your delivery make the words come alive with their intended and unintended meaning alike.

With each practice session, refine your artistry. Fondly embrace the duality of satire and irony and become a master of wielding their power. Trust your judgement here, and once you feel you are ready, step out into the world, armed with your newfound skills, and let your grumpy brilliance shine and the world quake beneath your grumpy feet.

The 3rd Element: Observational Grumpiness

As you continue to stand before your mirror, my seasoned grump, let us take a closer look at observational grumpiness. Here we will work on training your senses and cultivating a keen eye for the irritants that surround us in this ever-changing world. This is not a mere exercise in observation but a defiant stand against the ways of the younger generations... pfft, damn kids.

I can give you the building blocks here, and we can make observations about how dirty that mirror is or how the toilet paper roll was inserted upside down, but the true forum of observation lies out in the world populated with everyday fools. You can take the lessons you learn here to train yourself to spot the idiosyncrasies and quirks that others overlook. The things that really grate on your seasoned grumpy soul, like new modern trends and unneeded technologies that just complicate things, crazy styles and that god forsaken new 'music.' The outside world is literally filled like an endless sea with ridiculousness just waiting to be plucked off the giving tree.

Look for opportunities to expose and express your grumpy frustrations, injecting them into the flow of dialogue with a touch of seasoned wisdom. Your observations of these irritants will naturally seep into your conversations like a relentless drumbeat. It could be a disdainful comment about the reliance on smartphones or a simple remark about the superiority of "our" music. Whatever the observation, it's a dish best served cold with a comparative side dish consisting of "the way it used to be was better."

By seamlessly integrating your grumpy observations, you transform everyday encounters into grumpy tales of the past versus the present, the past being vastly superior... I know it, you know it. It's time for those damn kids to know it. If their parents did a good job raising them, they will thank you for your sage wisdom and realize just how right you are... sadly, don't expect this. With each observation shared, you will leave a lasting impression and become a master of observational grumpiness, educating those fortunate enough to engage in conversation with you.

The Grumpy Dialogue: Forging Connections through Discontent

Grumpy commentary should never be a solitary pursuit. Instead, seek out spirited grumpy dialogues with kindred spirits who appreciate the art of discontent. These encounters become more than just conversations; they are the battlegrounds where grumpy minds clash, inspire, and elevate one another. If you want to be the best, you have to compete with the best, and by compete I mean measure your grumpy yardsticks via grumpy dialogue.

In the realm of grumpy banter, finding a well-matched sparring partner is akin to discovering a rare gem. Together, you embark on a journey of mutual inspiration and challenge, fueling the flames of your grumpiness. In no time, you will create a dynamic synergy that elevates your discontent to new heights. In these dialogues, let your grumpy brilliance shine. Engage in verbal sparring that leaves no stone unturned, no societal absurdity unchallenged, no idiot unmocked. Take turns unleashing your biting wit, exchanging clever remarks and observations that evoke laughter, eye rolls, and nods of agreement. It is within these moments that grumpy camaraderie is born. Through the bond forged in grumpy banter, you will find solace, a shared understanding, and, above all, validation in your grumpy ideals.

Grumpy Targets and Etiquette: Grump Responsibly

In the realm of grumpy commentary, you must take aim with discernment and exercise steadfast restraint when necessary. While our discontent fuels our words, it is crucial to direct your verbal volleys at deserving targets. Choose wisely, focusing on the scenarios that warrant your grumpy input rather than launching indiscriminate attacks on individuals who don't deserve your grumpy wrath.

For example, imagine you find yourself at the supermarket, observing a young bagger learning the ropes. In such a situation, we must exercise understanding and give them a pass for the inevitable mistakes they may make. After all, they are on a journey of growth and should be applauded for their hard work.

However, picture an encounter with an overexuberant youth who mindlessly throws items into your grocery bag, completely oblivious to the delicate nature of your shopping, their earbuds blasting music as they pay no attention to the fact that they just placed a watermelon on top of your precious eggs. In this moment, the stage is set for your grumpy intervention.

It is important to recognize the distinction. Your grumpy commentary should be targeted at those who exhibit acts of carelessness or disregard or the like, rather than those who are genuinely trying their best. It's important to be a grump, not an asshole. Let us reserve our grumpy wrath for those deserving of our discontent, where our words can serve as a catalyst for their inevitable demise. Use well the skills you have learned here, and remember to interject any combination of facial expressions, sighs, and commentary—let it all fly. In order to not seem like a complete lunatic, it's best to start small and build to a resounding crescendo of crotchetiness.

Building Your Grumpy Repertoire

As we approach the culmination of this important journey through grumpy commentary, it is time to focus on building your grumpy repertoire. We shall explore three essential forms of grumpy expression, each with its own unique flavor and purpose. Prepare to expand your grumpy arsenal and leave a lasting impression on the world.

This is by no means an exhaustive list, just a starting point for you to hone your skills.

Form 1: The Quip - The Grumpy Arrow Shot from the Hip

Think of the quip like a verbal arrow shot straight from the hip. It is a quick, sharp retort that catches others off guard with its wit and brevity. Keep your quips at the ready, poised to strike whenever the opportunity arises. The key lies in delivering them with impeccable timing, leaving your target simultaneously amused and slightly wounded. In a matter of seconds, your grumpy quip can leave a lasting impression, evoking laughter and grudging admiration. This is a not a takedown shot but rather a swift and subtle jab. It is a passing quote, comment, or witty remark that leaves the recipient momentarily stunned, unsure of how to respond. As your target reels from the impact of your grumpy arrow, their amusement mixes with a tinge of wounded pride. They may even find themselves chuckling begrudgingly, unable to deny the cleverness of your retort. Job well done.

Form 2: The Grumpy Rant - Unleashing the Floodgates of Frustration

Ah, the grumpy rant, one of life's true indulgences, a glorious release of pent-up frustration that knows no bounds. It's that exhilarating moment when we unleash the floodgates of discontent, giving voice to our grievances with a ferocity that cannot be contained. Let your words surge forth like an unstoppable tempest, obliterating the annoyances of the world and leaving behind a trail of shattered complacency and a sense of relief and vindication.

Let there be no filters or inhibitions. It's your opportunity to express yourself with unadulterated and unapologetic grumpiness. Find the perfect balance between rawness and eloquence, ensuring that every word carries the weight of your discontent. As the floodgates burst open, let your frustrations pour forth with unbridled intensity, tearing down the walls of indifference that surround you.

In the echoes of your words, find liberation and empowerment, knowing that you are not alone in your grumpy perspective. Even if you stand alone in the room, your grumpy rant reverberates with the shared frustrations of fellow grumps through the ages. It's a thunderous chorus of discontent that demands to be heard, and damn the consequences.

Form 3: The Satirical Essay - Dissecting Absurdities with Grumpy Intellect

A playground for grumpy souls to unleash their discontent with the eloquence of a grumpy Shakespeare, Dive into the realm of absurdity and let your pen dance with wicked delight as you expose the follies of society. There's no room for reflection or lofty ideals here—just pure, unadulterated grumpiness expressed through the art of satire.

Summon your inner grumpy bard and weave words with the finesse of a master storyteller. Craft narratives that teeter on the edge of insanity, laced with biting wit and a touch of madness. Embrace the absurdity of life and channel your discontent into scathing observations that leave readers gasping for breath amidst fits of grumpy laughter and pearl clutching alike.

Let your satirical essay be a torrent of grumpy discontent, a tempest of words that shakes the foundations of convention. Spare no one from your razor-sharp quill as you skewer the absurdities that plague our existence. With every stroke, revel in the joy of your grumpy prose, knowing that you are giving voice to the frustrations that dwell within the grumpy corners of your soul.

Forging Your World-Class Grumpy Legacy

As a grumpy old man, you possess the power to craft a personal legacy of unparalleled grumpiness, a testament to your unique brand of disgruntlement. It is your solemn duty to etch your mark upon the annals of grumpy history, leaving behind a lasting impression for all to behold.

Embrace this noble quest, my brother, and unleash the full force of your grumpy prowess. Cultivate your own voice of grumpy authority, honing your skills with relentless determination. Remember to share your acumen with those who dare to traverse the path of discontent, inspiring them to embrace their own grumpy destinies.

In this journey, observation becomes your ally as you scrutinize the absurdities of the world with a discerning eye. Timing becomes your weapon as you deliver biting remarks and scathing retorts with impeccable precision. Let your discontented spirit soar, unfettered by societal norms, and unleash a torrent of grumpy brilliance upon the world.

By forging your world-class grumpy legacy, you ensure that your mark will be etched in the annals of grumpiness for all eternity. Each grumpy word, each scowl, and each sigh becomes a testament to your unrivaled grumpy greatness. Embrace the power within you and seize the opportunity to leave a cantankerous legacy that will be remembered and revered by future generations. You deserve it.

Continuing Education in Grumpiness

As we conclude this first volume, we have laid the foundation for your transition from middle aged and successful to old and grumpy. We have made huge strides learning the fundamentals and advanced facial expressions, many variations of grumpy sighs and the differences between them, and finished up on grumpy commentary, learning the various ways to communicate your grouchy disposition.

It's still a wide-open world out there, but fear not, for our adventure has only just begun! In the next volume, we shall venture into the enchanting realms of grumpy hobbies and adventures, where we seek solace and joy amidst the chaos of the world.

Until we meet again, may your days be filled with exasperation and your nights with mumbled complaints. Embrace the grumpy journey with unyielding resolve, for together we shall navigate the treacherous waters of grumpiness and emerge victorious, leaving a trail of eye rolls and bemused expressions in our wake. Onward we march, my fellow grump, to new horizons of grumpy enlightenment!

Printed in Great Britain
by Amazon

34823321R00030